For Poppy Isabella McGrath. J.W.

For Llewelyn Thomas Seddon Oliver. A.R.

Also by Jeanne Willis and Adrian Reynolds:

I'M SURE I SAW A DINOSAUR

MINE'S BIGGER THAN YOURS!

THAT'S NOT FUNNY!

UPSIDE DOWN BABIES

WHO'S IN THE LOO?

FSC
www.fsc.org

MIX
Paper from
responsible sources
FSC® C012700

First published in Great Britain in 2015 by Andersen Press Ltd.,
20 Vauxhall Bridge Road, London SW1V 2SA.
Published in Australia by Random House Australia Pty.,
Level 3, 100 Pacific Highway, North Sydney, NSW 2060.
Text copyright © Jeanne Willis, 2015.
Illustration copyright © Adrian Reynolds, 2015
The rights of Jeanne Willis and Adrian Reynolds to be
identified as the author and illustrator of this work
have been asserted by them in accordance with the
Copyright, Designs and Patents Act, 1988.
Colour separated in Switzerland by Photolitho AG, Zürich.
Printed and bound in Malaysia by Tien Wah Press.

10   9   8   7   6   5   4   3   2   1

British Library Cataloguing in Publication Data available.
ISBN 978 1 78344 039 9

READY, STEADY, JUMP!

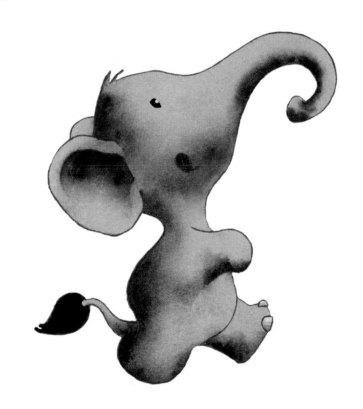

JEANNE WILLIS
ADRIAN REYNOLDS

ANDERSEN PRESS

Lions can jump.

Monkeys can jump.

Even giraffes can jump . . .

. . . but elephants can't.
"Why not?" asked Elephant.

"It's just the way we're made," said his mother.
"Something to do with our knees," said his father.
"Among other things," said his auntie.

But Elephant wouldn't give up.
"If I ran fast enough, I could jump
over that log," he thought.

So he ran his very fastest and . . .

. . . went tail over trunk.

"Elephants can't jump!" laughed Monkey.
"If I had something to bounce off, I could,"
thought Elephant.

So he found something bouncy.

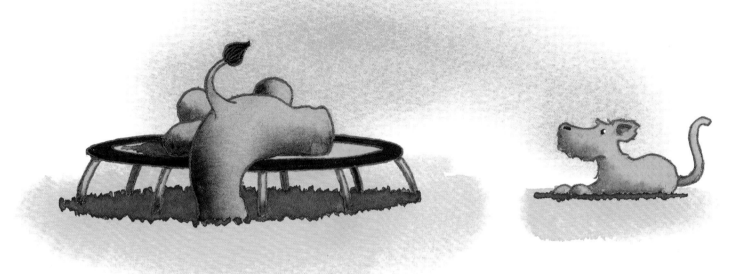

But no matter how hard he tried to jump up . . .

. . . he stayed down.

"Elephants can't jump!" laughed Lion.
"Maybe I could jump off something high,"
thought Elephant.

So he climbed to the top of a hill and he went,
"Ready, steady . . . **whoops!**"

"Elephants can't jump!" laughed Giraffe.

"Perhaps I could if I wasn't so heavy," thought Elephant.
So he had no dinner for **five** whole days.
Then he tried again. One, two, **three**, **jump** . . .

"Elephants can't jump!" all the animals laughed.

Elephant gave up.
He ate and ate, and got
bigger and **bigger**.

But he still felt very small on the inside.

Elephant went up a mountain to sulk.

But when he looked down, he saw a boy
who had fallen onto a rock below.

"Help!" cried the boy.

"Jump down and save me!"

"Elephants can't jump. I'll save you," said Monkey. Monkey jumped, but the boy was too heavy to lift and he was too scared to let go of Monkey.

"I'll jump down and save you," said Lion.
But the boy clung to Monkey, and when Monkey
climbed onto Lion, Lion couldn't jump back.

"Help!" they cried.

"I'll save you!" cried Giraffe, jumping down.
"Grab my neck, boy!"
But the boy was too scared. He clung to Monkey,
Monkey clung to Lion and Lion clung to Giraffe.

"Help, we're going to fall!" they cried.
"We can't save you!"

Suddenly, Elephant found his own
strength. He reached out with his long,
strong trunk and wrapped it around
Giraffe. Giraffe clung to Lion, Monkey
clung to the boy. Elephant pulled with
all his mighty **might** and . . .

They were so happy to be saved that they jumped **up** and **down**.

Elephant couldn't. But that didn't matter because he had done something no other animal could do. Not even Lion or Monkey or Giraffe.

Elephant was a **hero!**

"**Hooray** for Elephant!" everyone cheered.

And although Elephant kept his feet firmly on the ground . . .

. . . his heart **jumped** for **joy!**